D0575804

NATURE

By Heather Amery

A GOLDEN BOOK · NEW YORK

Western Publishing Company, Inc., Racine, Wisconsin 53404

Printed in Italy

© 1994 Reed International Books Limited. All rights
reserved. First published in Great Britain in 1993
by Hamlyn Children's Books, an imprint of Reed
Children's Books Limited, Michelin House, 81 Fulham
Road, London SW3 6RB, England. No part of this book
may be reproduced or copied in any form without
written permission from the publisher. All trademarks
are the property of Western Publishing Company, Inc.
Library of Congress Catalog Card Number: 93-73528
ISBN: 0-307-15663-X/ISBN: 0-307-65663-2 (lib. bdg.)
A MCMXCIV

Printed and bound in Italy by L.E.G.O. s.p.a.

CONTENTS

INTRODUCTION

Look closely at the world around you. All sorts of small things you might never have noticed before—a grain of sugar, a tiny insect, a speck of dust—may come into view. And if you use a magnifying glass, you will surely see even more.

Microscopes that use light and have several glass magnifying lenses were invented nearly 400 years ago. For the first time, scientists could see the germs that cause disease, the countless cells in our blood, and millions of other things that no one knew existed. Modern light-using microscopes can magnify an object up to 1,000 times its normal size.

We can look even more closely at the world with electron microscopes, which were invented about 60 years ago. Instead of using light, electron microscopes use a beam of electrons to "look" at tiny things, magnifying them up to 200,000 times.

In this book you will get a close-up look at many of the plants and small animals—of land, air, and sea—that inhabit our world.

Magnifications in this book are generally given beneath the pictures and consist of a multiplication sign followed by a number. For example, x 25 means the object is shown at 25 times its actual size. Where there is no magnification given, the photo is simply an enlargement.

▲ The researcher above is using an electron microscope to examine a tiny object. The magnified pictures show up on a television screen.

▼ The technician below is using a light microscope to study samples of bacteria.

▼ Look closely at a spoonful of sugar, and you can see that each grain is a roughly shaped crystal.

▶ Sugar as it is usually seen.

◀ Magnified 25 times (x 25), sugar resembles a collection of diamonds.

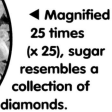

◀ At 50 times their normal size, these sugar crystals look like boulders.

◀ Here is the corner of a sugar crystal magnified 500 times.

Foraminifera shells
(x 60)

▲ These are the shells of very simple sea animals called foraminifera. Each one is about as big as a point on a pencil.

Diatoms

WATERY WORLD

Chock-full of tiny living things, the salty sea has an especially rich layer of microscopic plants and animals known as plankton floating just below its surface. Some types of plankton are the size of the dot on this *i*, and these are the giants of the plankton world! Most plankton are so small they can be seen only under a microscope, and several hundred could fit on the head of a pin. Freshwater ponds, lakes, and rivers contain an abundance of life as well.

▼ **All kinds of algae.** Algae are plants that live in water. There are thousands of different types of algae, and they come in an incredible variety of shapes and sizes—everything from little balls, flat disks, and tiny pyramids to long needles and pointed stars. Many have hairs or spines to help them float. Others attach themselves to rocks in the water.

One type of algae that lives both in the sea and in fresh water is the diatom. There are more than 10,000 different kinds of diatoms. The name means "cut through," and it fits these plants perfectly because diatoms live inside glassy shells that appear to have been cut in half. In warm seas, over 1,000 of them may be found in a single cup of water.

◄ When diatoms are magnified, their glassy shells look like precious gems.

BILLIONS OF FORAMINIFERA SHELLS HAVE BEEN COMPRESSED OVER MILLIONS OF YEARS TO FORM HUGE WHITE CLIFFS.

◀ This is the skeleton of a radiolarian, a tiny animal that lives inside the plankton.

(x 700)

Plague of plankton. Many sea animals depend on plankton for food. But too much plankton can be a problem. Certain types of reddish-colored plankton breed very quickly, until there are so many of them that they turn the water red. Sometimes these so-called red tides are harmless, but other times they produce poisons that kill everything else in the water. When this happens, other creatures that feed on sea life become sick or die, too. During one red tide off the coast of South America, the number of seabirds dropped from about 30 million to 5 million. A red tide can cover an area in the sea as big as the state of Rhode Island.

Radiolarian skeletons

(x 265)

▶ This picture shows the structure of a radiolarian skeleton. Radiolarians have lived in the sea for millions of years.

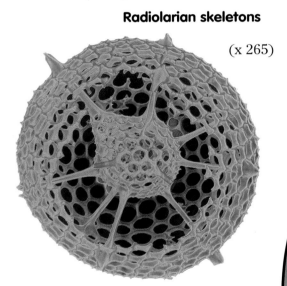

DID YOU KNOW?

A certain type of plant plankton produces flashes of light. When the water is churned up by wind or waves, the plankton make the sea sparkle. If there are masses of these plankton in the water, the light they make can be bright enough for a person to read by.

▶ This strange watery ball is not one single creature but several, all living together in a floating colony. The creature is called a volvox. Volvox colonies are found in freshwater lakes and ponds.

Colony of volvox
(x 200)

FLOWER POWER

(x 1.5)

Dandelion florets

About 250,000 different types of flowers exist in the world. This huge number does not include all the ones that have been specially bred for their colors and scents in gardens and greenhouses. Flowers bloom almost everywhere on earth—even in the frozen Arctic and the hottest, driest deserts.

(x 10)

Beautiful blooms. Most flowers have a ring of special leaves called sepals, which surround and protect the bud. Inside them a ring of colorful petals surrounds the seed-making parts of the plant. The brilliant colors and sweet scents of flowers attract bees, butterflies, flies, and other insects, as well as land animals and birds. These "visitors" help the plants not only to make new seeds but also to carry the seeds to different places.

◄ A close look at a dandelion flower shows that it is actually a cluster of many tiny flowers, or florets. One flower head may contain as many as 200 florets.

(x 60)

THE BIGGEST FLOWER IN THE WORLD IS THE RAFFLESIA. FOUND IN SOUTHEAST ASIA, IT IS OVER 3 FEET ACROSS AND SMELLS LIKE ROTTING MEAT—THE PERFECT PERFUME TO ATTRACT FLIES.

► Flower petals look and feel smooth, but this close-up of a chickweed petal shows it has rows of closely packed vertical cells.

Chickweed petal
(x 240)

Chickweed
(x 8)

▲ **Tiny tempters.** Tiny chickweed flowers are only about 1/3 of an inch across. The flowers have five green sepals on the outside and five petals on the inside, each split down the middle. The bright color of the petals attracts many kinds of insects.

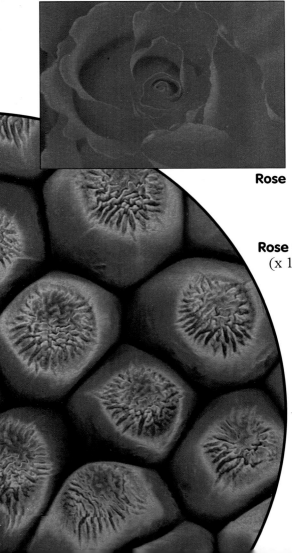

Rose

Rose petal
(x 1,000)

◄ A rose's rich color may be due to the way the rounded cells on the surface of each petal reflect light.

DID YOU KNOW?

Like landing lights on an airport runway, the markings that appear on flower petals serve as guides for bees. They indicate where the pollen supply is and where any new pollen that the bees are carrying should be dropped off.

Herb Robert stamens (x 5)

▲ In the center of this herb Robert wildflower, five stamens are just releasing their pollen. On the petals around them are five more stamens, which will soon produce more pollen.

STIGMAS AND STAMENS

No matter how beautiful they look or smell, flowers are just one stage in the way some plants reproduce themselves. Seed making actually takes place deep within the petals, through a process called pollination. Only a flower that has been pollinated can produce seeds that will grow into the next generation of plants.

▶ **The birds and the bees.** Although they may look very different, all flowers have the same basic parts. The male part, called the stamen, produces pollen. The female part, called the stigma, receives the pollen that pollinates, or fertilizes, the seeds in the plant's ovary.

Although some plants can fertilize themselves, most can only be fertilized by pollen from another plant of the same kind. Insects, bees, and wind carry pollen from one plant to another. The animals come for the nectar, a sugary liquid produced by the plants. The sticky pollen clings to their bodies as they feed and is carried away when they fly off.

Chickweed stamens and stigmas (x 12)

Anther of a crown-of-thorns flower (x 125)

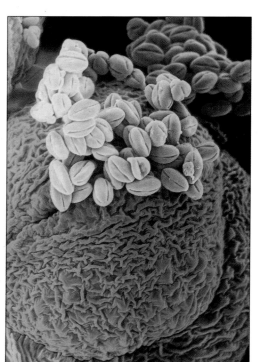

◀ The orange anther on this crown-of-thorns flower has split open, exposing its yellow pollen grains. The anther, which is on the top part of a stamen, produces the pollen.

USUALLY A PLANT CANNOT FERTILIZE ITSELF, BECAUSE THE FLOWER'S MALE AND FEMALE PARTS DO NOT MATURE AT THE SAME TIME.

DID YOU KNOW?

Bucket orchids produce a nectar that makes bees drunk. The drunken bees then fall into a pool of water inside the petals. The orchid's pollen sticks to the bees as they struggle to escape, increasing the chances that pollen will reach other bucket orchids.

▶ Pollen grains develop inside the anther of a shepherd's purse flower. When the anther is mature, it splits open and releases the pollen.

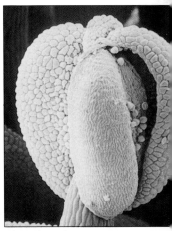

Shepherd's purse anther
(x 100)

Drop of nectar on a chickweed flower
(x 45)

▲ At the base of a chickweed flower's long stamens, on the sides, are drops of nectar. The picture to the left shows the center of a chickweed flower. In the middle are the stigmas, which have been fertilized by pollen from the stamens.

▶ **A matter of luck.** Orchard grass is grown in fields to feed cows, sheep, and other farm animals. It has branches of tufted flowers. Yellow pollen carried from another plant by the wind has collected on this orchard grass flower's orange stigma.

When pollen from a plant is carried off by the wind, there is no guarantee that any of it will land on another flower of the same plant. To increase the odds of this happening, plants that are wind-pollinated produce huge amounts of pollen, much of which is wasted. Some trees, most grasses, and a few small flowering plants are pollinated this way.

Orchard grass flower
(x 30)

GOLDEN GRAINS

Pollen in your hand looks like fine yellow dust. If you examine it under a high-powered microscope, though, you will see an amazing variety of sizes, shapes, and textures. The most common shape is a kind of stretched-out circle called an ellipse. About half the flowering plants in the world produce ellipse-shaped pollen. But pollen can also be either perfectly round, elongated into thin rods, or many-sided.

DID YOU KNOW?

Cucumber pollen grains measure only 8/1,000 of an inch across, but these are the giants of the plant pollen world. The tiniest grains, like those of the alpine forget-me-not, are less than 12/10,000 of an inch across.

Orchard grass pollen
(x 850)

▲ The pollen grain above is typical of wind-pollinated plants. Its smooth surface keeps it from sticking to other grains.

▶ **Truly indestructible.** The outer casing of a pollen grain is like a suit of armor. Pollen grains dropped into acid or heated to very high temperatures remain completely unharmed.

Fossilized pollen grains are common. The surface patterns of many different pollen grains have been found imprinted in clay, coal, limestone, and sandstone. These fossils show us exactly what kinds of plants grew on earth hundreds or even thousands of years ago.

Pot marigold pollen
(x 1,600)

▲ The tiny barbs on pot marigold pollen hook on to an insect's body.

ONE SPIKE OF A BIRCH TREE CAN PRODUCE OVER 5 MILLION GRAINS OF YELLOW POLLEN.

Artful arrangement. Some flowers are very carefully designed to make sure that as much pollen as possible is picked up by visitors. Honeysuckle flowers are simply long tubes made of two petals. Their color and strong scent attract butterflies and moths. To get to the sweet nectar, the insects have to reach down into the flower. In the process, they can't help brushing against the well-positioned stamens.

Honeysuckle flowers

▶ **Chemical coding.** Each type of pollen has its own special proteins. If the right proteins reach the right stigma, the pollen grain pushes down through the stigma to where the female cells, or ovules, are stored. The male cell in the pollen grain then joins with an ovule to form a seed.

Pollen on goosegrass stigmas
(x 1,750)

Nose ticklers

If your eyes start tearing and you can't stop sneezing on a lovely spring day, you may have a cold, but more likely you have hay fever. That means you are allergic to the pollen in the air. Don't worry. As soon as the flowers stop producing pollen, you can breathe easy again.

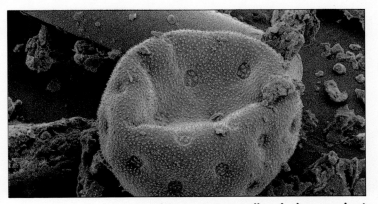

Lamb's-quarter pollen in house dust
(x 4,300)

A SEEDY BUSINESS

All flowering plants produce seeds. Given the right soil and favorable conditions, the seeds will sprout and grow into new plants that loosely resemble the parent plants. Many plants use wind, water, animals, and birds in special ways to spread their seeds so that as many of them as possible will have a chance to grow. Some plants even have exploding pods that shoot seeds over the ground.

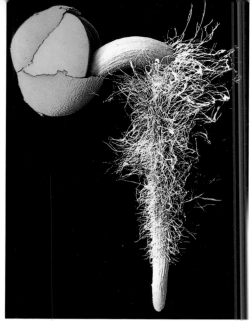

Cabbage seed
(x 8)

▲ When a seed starts to grow, it takes in water and its hard shell splits open. The root then pushes out, sprouting fine hairs as it grows.

Poppy seed pod

Poppy seeds

◄ **Pods a-poppin'.** On the left are two views of the seed pod of a corn poppy flower. The flower petals have died and fallen off, leaving the dry pod. As soon as the seeds inside are ripe, the pod splits open at the top. When the pod is shaken by the wind, the dark seeds sprinkle down onto the ground.

All seeds contain a supply of food to nurture them while they grow. The seed's hard shell protects it as it lies on the ground during the winter. When spring comes, bringing rain and warm weather, the seed begins to sprout.

▼ The poppies below are at different stages of growth. Some have unopened buds, some are in full flower, and some have ripening seed pods.

Gotcha!

Some plants have sticky seeds or burrs that hook on to animal fur, bird feathers, or human clothing as it brushes against the plant. The burr later drops off—sometimes miles away from the parent plant.

Hook on a goosegrass burr
(x 150)

Animal aid. The seeds in berries, fruits, and nuts are carried away from trees by birds and other animals. Some animals eat fruit that falls to the ground. The fruit seeds pass through the animals' gut and come out in their droppings. Other animals, such as squirrels, collect nuts to eat or store but then drop them or forget where they hid them.

DID YOU KNOW?

The seed pods of Himalayan balsams explode when an animal brushes against them or when a strong wind blows on them. The pods split open and expel the seeds, which may land more than three feet away from the plant.

◀ **The tiny snapdragon seed has a very rough case. When it falls to the ground, the ridges and pits get caught in the soil and keep the seed from being blown away by the wind.**

Snapdragon seed
(x 65)

UP TO **20,000** SEEDS ARE PRODUCED BY ONE ORCHID FLOWER. THE SEEDS ARE SO LIGHT THAT A MILLION WOULD WEIGH ONLY AS MUCH AS ONE BAKED BEAN!

LUSCIOUS LEAVES

Leaves grow in every shape and size. The floating duckweed's leaves are only as big as a pinprick. The leaves of the raffia palm are as long as a bus. The leaf's size and shape depends on where it grows and what sort of weather it is exposed to. Plants use their leaves like solar panels to collect sunlight, so those found in dark forests look very different from those found in deserts or on windy mountaintops.

Hairs on a sea buckthorn leaf
(x 80)

▲ The undersides of sea buckthorn leaves are covered with tiny hairs. Scientists think these hairs prevent the leaves from drying out on the windy seashore.

Closed tobacco leaf pores
(x 580)

▶ The pores on a tobacco leaf open during the day and close at night and in very dry weather.

▶ **The meaning of green.** Most leaves are green because they contain a green chemical called chlorophyll. In sunlight, a plant's leaves take in carbon dioxide gas from the air. The leaves use their chlorophyll to change the carbon dioxide and water taken up by the plant's roots into the food the plant needs to grow. The leaves also give off oxygen through tiny pores. The whole process is called photosynthesis, which means "putting together with light."

At night, when it is dark, green plants reverse the process, taking in oxygen and giving out carbon dioxide.

Open tobacco leaf pores
(x 470)

DID YOU KNOW?

Green plants produce all of the oxygen there is in the world, putting out more of it during the day than they take in at night. Without green plants, the oxygen in the air would be slowly used up, and all the people and animals would die.

Lavender

Oil-secreting glands on lavender leaves
(x 120)

◄ **Lavender has tough, narrow leaves. The flowering shoots produce a sweet-scented oil that is used to make perfume. In the past, lavender was also used in medicines.**

► **Masses of moss.** Mosses are simple green plants that grow in thick cushions almost everywhere. They cling to roofs and walls but prefer the rocks and trees in woodlands and other damp places. Mosses are the first plants to grow on bare rocks. Soil and dead leaves blown by the wind collect around them, making a bed where the seeds of flowering plants can grow. Mosses have stems and leaves but no flowers.

New moss grows from small reproductive cells called spores, which are released from special capsules like the one on the right. The fringelike strands around the mouth of this capsule are sensitive to water in the air. They release spores according to the amount of moisture they detect.

Moss capsule
(x 215)

SOME PLANTS, SUCH AS HOLLY TREES, HAVE SHARP SPINES ON THEIR LEAVES TO KEEP HUNGRY ANIMALS AWAY.

In Self-Defense

Plants are always in danger of being eaten. Tiny insects suck sap from their stems, caterpillars chew their leaves, birds peck at their seeds, grubs burrow into their roots, and large grazing animals gobble them right down to the ground. Some species of plants survive merely because there are so many of them, but others defend themselves with prickles, stingers, or poisons. A few plants even eat some of their attackers.

◄ Stinging nettles grow along the edges of fields and roads. Grazing animals know to leave them alone unless they are cut down by humans and can no longer sting.

Stinging nettles

▶ **Poisoned points.** The leaves of the stinging nettle have long hairs that end in brittle tips made of a hard material called silica. When an animal brushes against a leaf, the tips break off and the sharp point jabs into the animal's skin. Pressure at the base of the leaf hair forces poison out through the point. The poison causes an itchy red rash, which soon fades. If nettle leaves are grabbed very firmly, the tips of the hairs break off, but the points only bend and so do not release their poison. In the past, people ate boiled nettles as a vegetable and used the dried leaves to make tea.

Hairs on a stinging nettle leaf (x 135)

Stinging nettle hair (x 95)

◄ This stinging nettle leaf hair has a drop of poison at its tip. Thousands of tiny hairs cover stinging nettle leaves, but only the long ones carry poison.

MANY CACTI ARE COVERED WITH SHARP SPINES TO DISCOURAGE DESERT ANIMALS FROM EATING THEIR JUICY LEAVES.

DID YOU KNOW?

The Venus's-flytrap eats insects and even small frogs. Some of the plant's leaves fold over like jaws. When an insect lands on the sensitive leaf hairs, the "jaws" snap shut, trapping the insect inside. The leaves open up again after the trespasser has been digested.

Sundew leaf tentacles
(x 60)

▼ **Sundew plants have long red tentacles, each with a blob of sticky liquid at the end. The blob shines like dew in the sun, giving the plant its name.**

Fly on a sundew leaf
(x 20)

▲ **Sticky situation.** The Venus's-flytrap is just one of several plants that eat insects and small animals. Most grow in wet, boggy ground where there are few plants or animals to enrich the soil with their dead leaves, droppings, and carcasses. An occasional insect snack provides these plants with the extra nourishment they need.

Sundew plants use the tentacles on their leaves to trap insects. Any passing insect that is attracted by the gluelike liquid on the tentacles soon finds itself stuck. The tentacles bend inward, forcing the insect against the leaves in the center. The tentacles then produce more liquid, which drowns and digests the insect.

Sundew leaves

THE ROOT OF THE MATTER

Plant roots have two main jobs. They must hold the plant firmly in the soil so that it isn't blown away by the wind, washed away by the rain, or pulled up by a feeding animal. Roots must also absorb water and mineral salts from the ground to feed the growing plant. Some big roots, such as those of carrots, are actually food the plants have stored away.

Wheat root
(x 40)

▲ The root of a wheat plant produces a thin slime that helps the tip slide easily through the soil as it grows downward. The cells that produce the slime are constantly shed, and new ones grow in their place to protect the growing root tip.

▼ Soaking it up. Plants use their roots to get water from the soil. Soil is made up of tiny particles with air spaces between them. A thin film of water surrounds each particle. To get at this water, roots have finer roots on them—root hairs—usually at the tips. These root hairs direct water to the roots, where it collects in special tubes called xylem vessels *(see cross section below)*. The water moves up the xylem vessels and into the plant's stem.

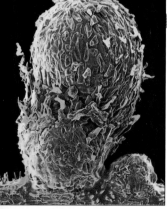

Nodule on a pea root
(x 10)

▲ Some bacteria form a special relationship with plant roots. In return for being allowed to live on the roots (in growths called nodules), the bacteria take nitrogen gas from the air and turn it into a natural fertilizer.

Xylem vessels in a broad bean root
(x 235)

ONION BULBS ARE THE ONION PLANT'S STORE OF SUGAR. IT IS THE SUGAR THAT MAKES ONIONS TURN BROWN WHEN THEY ARE FRIED.

Send down some air. All roots must be able to breathe. Most take in air from the soil. Water lilies have other ways of getting air. So do other plants with roots that grow in the bottom of ponds, lakes, streams, and rivers. Their leaves have large air holes that are joined to large air tubes in the stems. These tubes lead down to the underwater roots.

Star-shaped structures line the air holes of water lily leaves. These structures contain masses of poisonous crystals—a good defense against burrowing insects.

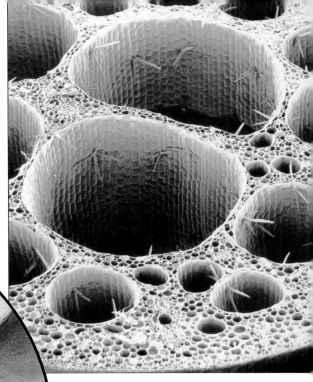

Water lily stem
(x 14)

▲ Air fills the large hollow tubes of water lily stems *(shown in the cross section above)*. This helps the stems float in the water.

Lining of an air hole in a water lily leaf
(x 100)

◄ Tubelike vessels in the stem of a pea plant transport water to the leaves. The spiral pattern around it makes the vessel strong and helps give the plant its shape.

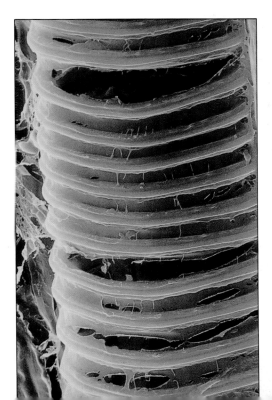

Water-transporting vessel in a pea stem
(x 600)

DID YOU KNOW?

Ivy and other plants that climb up walls and trees hang on with hundreds of tiny roots that grow from their stems. The roots take nothing from the bark of the trees and do not harm them. They just use them for support.

Fly agaric toadstools

FASCINATING FUNGI

Unlike other plants, fungi lack chlorophyll. Fungi get their food from rotting leaves, animal manure, the remains of dead animals, or living plants and animals. There are thousands of different kinds of fungi. They range from the molds that grow on cheese and stale bread to mushrooms and toadstools that grow in fields and woods.

▲ **Fly agaric toadstools are poisonous and grow in the woods. Their poison was once used to make fly traps, which is how they got their name.**

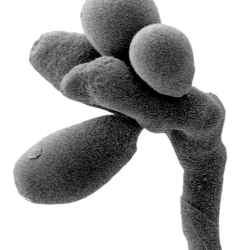

Mushroom spores
(x 5,400)

◄ **Fungi fruits.** Unlike green plants, a fungus does not have roots, stems, leaves, or flowers. Instead it has a mass of very fine threads that grow through whatever the fungus is feeding on. The larger fungi, the mushrooms and toadstools, spread their threads underground. Before they reproduce, the threads bunch up into knobs and become covered with a cap. These pop out of the ground very quickly, sometimes overnight. Mushrooms and toadstools are called fruiting bodies, and they produce tiny spores instead of seeds. The wind blows the spores away, and if they land in the right type of soil, they grow into new fungi.

Fruiting body of a seed fungus
(x 5,000)

◄ **Threads of one fungus grow on the seeds of cereals and grasses (far left). The spores of this fungus develop inside the four yellow pear-shaped knobs on the fruiting body (near left).**

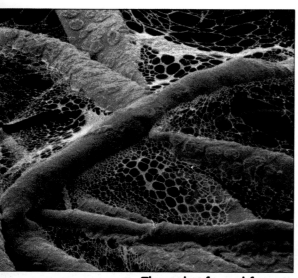

Threads of seed fungus
(x 8,200)

◄ This fungus, which sometimes infects human ears, making them red and itchy, grows in soil and on rotting plants. The brown balls on the ends of the blue threads are the spores.

Soil fungus
(x 260)

DID YOU KNOW?

Fairy rings, the dark green rings that sometimes appear in circular patches in grass, are made by a fungus. As the threads of the fungus spread outward, the dying fungus from the middle fertilizes the soil, making the grass there a deeper green. People once believed that these rings were the dancing places of fairies.

Potato blight

◄ When potato blight attacks a potato plant, the threads of the fungus grow into the pores of the leaves, causing them to wilt and die.

► The destroyers. Some fungi live on plants and fruits, damaging and destroying them. Wheat, rice, oat, and barley plants, as well as some roots and trees, may be attacked by fungi. The fungi spores live in the soil or in a plant during the winter. When the plant begins to grow in the spring, so does the fungus. The fungus may quickly produce spores that are then spread by wind and water to new homes in the growing crops. About 150 years ago, the potato crop in Ireland was destroyed four years in a row by a fungus called potato blight. More than a million Irish people starved to death and about half a million left the country in search of food, largely because their English rulers kept the other crops for themselves.

Threads of potato blight
(x 1,300)

A LARGE MUSHROOM PRODUCES ABOUT 15 BILLION SPORES, BUT ONLY A FEW WILL GROW INTO NEW FUNGI.

WATER BABIES

If you were asked to draw an adult starfish, you would probably start with the five arms that give it its shape. If you were asked to draw a baby starfish, you'd most likely draw the same thing, only smaller. But you would be wrong. Starfish are one of a number of creatures that start life looking very different from their parents. Many of the larger "plankton" are really very young, or larval, forms of much more familiar creatures.

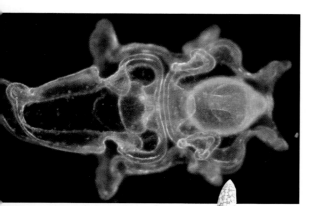

Starfish baby

▲ This tiny animal above will grow into an adult starfish. The bud at one end will develop after the new starfish settles on the bottom of the sea.

Starfish

Sea anemone

▼ **Strange changes.** Many of the small sea animals that start life swimming among plankton spend their adulthood standing or crawling on the sea floor, clinging to rocks or shells, or burrowing into the sand. Adult sea anemones, for example, usually stay attached to rocks. The female's eggs are fertilized by a male and hatch inside her. There they develop into tiny larvae, which swim out through her mouth and into the water. Later, when they settle on the bottom of the sea, the larvae change into tiny anemones. Sea urchins also begin life as free-swimming larvae. They eventually settle on the seabed, their hard round bodies covered with spines.

Sea urchin

◀ **Baby sea anemones** are almost transparent. This makes it very difficult for their enemies to spot them.

▲ Sea urchins have spines that help keep them afloat.

Sea anemone baby

Sea urchin baby

DID YOU KNOW?

There are about 10 million different kinds of small animals living on the bottom of the world's seas and oceans. About half of them produce babies that swim in the warmer waters near the surface.

▼ **This medusa is the second stage of an obelia's young. Depending on its sex, the medusa sheds eggs or sperm as it floats in the water.**

Medusa
(x 125)

▶ **All about obelias.** Another sea creature that has a different larval form is the obelia. This tiny animal produces its young in two stages. The obelia, which looks like a plant on the seabed, first grows a bud. Every so often a medusa—a curious, bell-shaped piece of jelly with many trailing tentacles—emerges from the bud. The medusa may be either male or female. If it is male, it swims off and releases sperm into the water. If it is female, it releases eggs. After an egg is fertilized by a sperm, it develops into a larva, which sinks to the seafloor and grows into an adult.

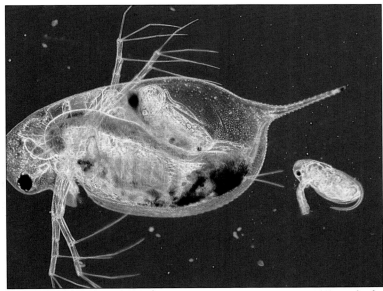

Daphnia
(x 30)

◀ **Family resemblance.** Not all tiny water creatures have unlikely looking young. This daphnia, a freshwater flea, has just given birth to a baby that is a miniature copy of itself. A small pond or lake may teem with daphnia, which provide food for many other animals. They are also fed to fish raised in tanks and aquariums.

WORM'S-EYE VIEW

Billions of small creatures live on our planet. These include the many thousands of types of snails and worms that live on dry land, in lakes, rivers, ponds, and in the sea. Though some are pests that attack and destroy food plants and crops, most are useful. They feed on rotting plants and dead animals, and by so doing put useful minerals back into the soil.

DID YOU KNOW?

When the tide comes in, a certain type of snail in southern Africa feeds on dead fish that have been washed up by the sea. The snail, using its foot like a surfboard, is swept along the shore to places where a meal might be found. When the tide goes out again, the snail hides in the sand until the next high tide.

▶ **A big bite.** Snails have tongues covered with rows of tiny, sharp teeth. Land snails use their rough tongues to break up pieces of green plants, fruit, dead earthworms and slugs, and other rotting matter.

All snails carry shells on their back. A snail's body is coiled up inside the shell. The only parts that appear outside are the head and the underneath part, which is called the foot.

Snail's tongue (x 880)

Giant African land snail

▶ Friends of the earth. Earthworms have no legs and no obvious heads or tails, but they get along fine without them. Their bodies, made up of many sections, have nearly invisible hairs. A worm moves by lengthening its front part and pushing through the soil, then pulling its hindquarters up. It uses its hairs to keep a grip on the soil as it moves. If the soil is packed down and has no cracks for the worm to crawl through, the worm eats its way along. Earthworms feed on dead and rotting plants. They enrich the soil with their droppings and with the dead leaves and twigs they pull down into their burrows. Their holes also make natural drainage channels for rainwater.

Common earthworm

Earthworm's head
(x 12)

Earthworm's skin
(x 34)

▼ Whelks, which are related to snails, also have a rough, toothy tongue. They use it to bore through the shells of other mollusks and eat the juicy insides.

▲ Earthworms eat large amounts of soil with their food. Some leave droppings, called worm casts, on the ground.

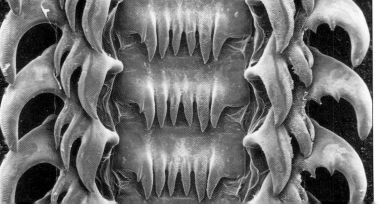

An earthworm that lives in Tasmania is as long as a bed and is said to make a gurgling noise as it inches along.

Whelk's tongue
(x 125)

SLEEK SWIMMERS

All fish, frogs, and toads belong to a group of animals known as vertebrates—animals with backbones—and so do all people. Fish were the very first vertebrates to appear on earth. The amphibians (frogs and toads) came next. There are now more than 25,000 different kinds of fish, ranging from tiny creatures only half an inch long to giant sharks of 50 feet, plus about 4,000 types of amphibians.

DID YOU KNOW?

A tree frog that lives in the South American rainforests releases a deadly poison from glands in its skin. This poison protects the tree frog from being eaten by snakes, lizards, and other predators. Native Indian hunters still use this poison. They cover their arrowheads with it to use in hunting small animals and birds.

▼ **These tadpoles of a map tree frog are swimming in a river on the Caribbean island of Trinidad. Unlike most tadpoles, they swim together in tight groups.**

▼ **Treetop hoppers.** Some types of frogs and toads live in trees. Sucker pads on their toes help them cling to the bark and leaves. Most spawn, or lay their eggs, in water. Others, which live in the tropical rainforests, spawn on leaves. When their tadpoles hatch, these frogs carry them to the tiny pools of rainwater that collect in some of the flowers. The tadpoles feed on insect eggs that float on the water's surface.

Toad's egg
(x 420)

Tree frog

Tree frog tadpoles

▶ **This ball of cells is the beginning of a new toad. In just one week it will have taken the shape of a tadpole, ready to wriggle free of its jelly into the water.**

THE BIGGEST FROG IN THE WORLD, CALLED THE GOLIATH FROG, IS ABOUT A FOOT LONG.

Fin feast

Many tiny, very simple animals called protozoans live in water. Some of these are parasites. Instead of hunting and catching food for themselves, they survive on the body fluids of a larger animal. The protozoan on the right is nibbling on a guppy's fin.

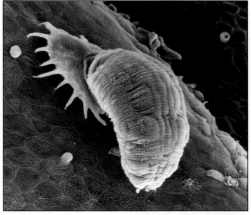

Protozoan
(x 350)

▶ **Scaly skin.** Almost all fish are covered from head to tail with a special kind of body armor—thousands and thousands of overlapping scales. The masheer fish, found in the rivers of India, has scales as large as a human hand, while the common eel's scales are so small they can be seen only with a microscope. In addition to protecting the fish, scales help streamline its body so it can move quickly and smoothly through water.

Dogfish scales
(x 48)

▶ **The triangular scales on a dogfish's skin all point toward its tail. This helps the fish swim forward but makes swimming backward very difficult.**

Tadpole

Dogfish

WINGS AND THINGS

◄ The shell of a bird's egg is a remarkable piece of animal engineering. It is very lightweight and punctured with tiny pores that allow the chick to breathe. The shell is so tough that it takes some baby birds more than a day to chip their way through to the outside world.

Chick hatching from egg

There are more than 8,500 kinds of birds in the world. They range from tiny lightweight hummingbirds to huge ostriches that are too heavy to fly. Birds live in every part of the world, from dense rainforests and hot deserts to muddy marshlands and the frigid polar regions. The only vertebrates that can fly are birds and bats. Birds' bodies have light, hollow bones and feathers to help them fly. The feathers also keep them warm and dry.

► **Feather features.** Birds are the only animals with feathers. The flight feathers, which are on their wings, are long and stiff, with strong but flexible shafts down the middle. Birds use these feathers to fly forward and to lift themselves up in the air. They use their tail feathers to steer. On the bird's body are feathers similar to flight feathers. These are called contour feathers, and they give the bird its shape.

The downy feathers under the outer layer keep the bird warm. Seabirds and birds that live in the cold polar regions have lots of these feathers. Some birds also have bristly feathers around their beaks, which help them to feed.

Down feathers
(x 25)

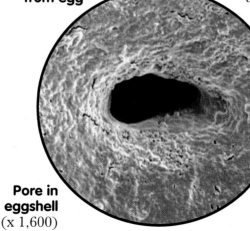

Pore in eggshell
(x 1,600)

Golden eagle

Zip! A bird's flight and contour feathers have hundreds of thin, soft "branches," called barbs, on each side of the shaft. The barbs hook together like the teeth on a zipper, making the feathers smooth and strong. When a feather gets bent out of shape, the bird strokes it back with its beak. A bird may have trouble flying if its flight feathers are broken or damaged. But if a whole feather is pulled out, a new one will grow back in about two months.

Look into my eyes!

The feathers of most male birds are much more colorful than those of the females. A peahen is a drab brown bird, but the peacock is dazzling. To attract a mate, the male shakes his 200 tail feathers— each with a brightly colored "eye." The female is apparently hypnotized by this glittering display.

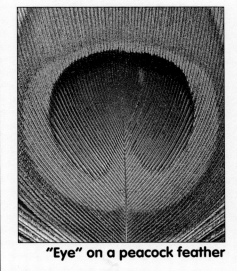

"Eye" on a peacock feather

▼ **A bird's hollow bones are light but strong. They have a honeycomb of air sacs that are linked to the bird's lungs.**

Barbs on a wing feather
(x 150)

Hollow bird bone
(x 80)

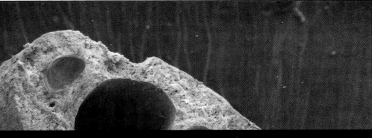

A WHISTLING SWAN HAS MORE FEATHERS THAN ANY OTHER BIRD—MORE THAN **25,000.** A RUBY-THROATED HUMMINGBIRD HAS ONLY **940.**

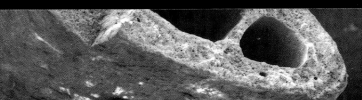

Winter snow in Utah

▲ When the temperature rises, water from melting snow on mountains turns streams and rivers into rushing torrents.

CRYSTAL CLEAR

All of the water in the world comes from the clouds in the sky. It falls as rain, snow, sleet, and hail. When rain reaches the ground, much of it runs into streams and rivers. The rest sinks into the earth, rising back to the surface in freshwater springs. The springs and streams join up to form rivers, which flow down to the sea. In the heat of the sun, water evaporates and turns into water vapor that rises up unseen in the air. When the vapor is cooled, it turns into tiny droplets of water that form new clouds in the sky. And so the water cycle begins again.

DID YOU KNOW?

When water freezes into ice, it gets bigger, or expands. The ice also gets lighter, which enables it to float on top of the water. If ice could not float, all the seas and oceans of the world would freeze solid, and nothing would be able to live on the earth.

▶ **Winter wonders.** Snow is water that has frozen into tiny crystals on pellets of ice in a cloud. As the crystals fall through the cloud, they bump into other crystals, joining together and growing bigger and bigger. If the air is cold enough, they fall to the ground as snowflakes. Otherwise, they melt on the way down and fall as rain. Hail is formed when ice crystals are blown or carried up and down in a cloud, collecting layers of ice until they become so heavy that they fall as hailstones.

Ice crystals
(x 1,200)

▼ **Brrr!** The tiny ice crystals that make up snowflakes come in different shapes and sizes. Most snowflakes have six sides, but the actual shape of the crystals depends on the temperature of the cloud in which they form. If it is very cold, the crystals join up to make rod and needle shapes. If it is somewhat warmer, the crystals take much more complicated shapes. Although billions of snowflakes fall from the clouds every year, no two have ever been found to be exactly alike.

Snowflakes
(x 70)

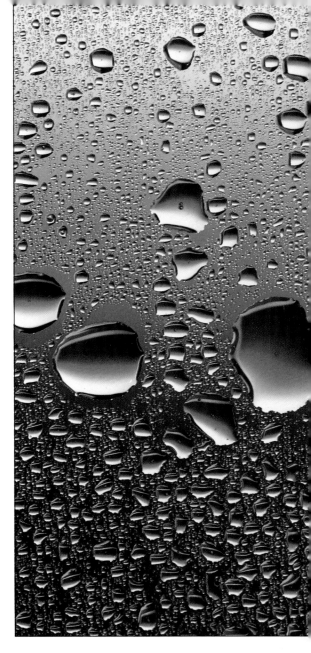

Water drops on a window

▶ Drops of water appear on windows, glasses of ice-cold drinks, and other cold surfaces when water vapor in the air cools and collects. This is called condensation.

▶ When the air is very cold, water vapor that has condensed onto a cold surface freezes into ice crystals. These crystals join up to make the ferny patterns of frost.

33

DOWN TO EARTH

Much of the world is covered with soil. It can vary from less than an inch to many feet thick. All life on earth depends on the soil. Plant-eating animals, including human beings, live on the food produced by plants that grow in it. Meat-eating animals feed on the animals that live on those plants. The soil also provides homes for an enormous number of small animals.

DID YOU KNOW?

Desert sand dunes can be over 800 feet high and more than 60 miles long. As the wind blows sand up one side of a dune and down the other, the dune creeps along, burying everything—even whole cities—in its path. In New Mexico, the snowlike dunes of the White Sands National Monument cover over 275 square miles.

Sand grains (x 20)

◄ **Rock bottom.** Both sand and soil are made from rock that has been eroded, or ground up, into very small pieces by wind, water, frost, and the heat of the sun over millions of years. Sand is found at the bottom of seas and shallow lakes, along shorelines, and in huge quantities in deserts. In different areas, different things are mixed in with the rock particles. On some tropical beaches you'll find that the sand appears to be just ground-up coral and tiny pieces of broken seashell worn smooth by erosion. Most beaches have at least some tiny shells mixed in with the billions of rock particles.

A tiny seashell *(center)* among **sand grains** (x 60)

▼ **Most sand is made from sandstone rock that has been eroded by glaciers or by rocks rubbing together, washed away by water, or worn away by the wind.**

Sandy beach

▶ **Worms at work.** Soil may look dead, but it teems with life. Masses of tiny animals and fungi are at work in the earth, usually in the topmost layers. The soil is constantly being enriched by the living things that depend on it for their existence. Leaves, fruits, and flowers as well as dead plants and fungi add nutrients to the soil so that the next generation of plants can grow. Animal droppings and the remains of dead animals rot away in it, adding useful minerals. Even bacteria help enrich the soil.

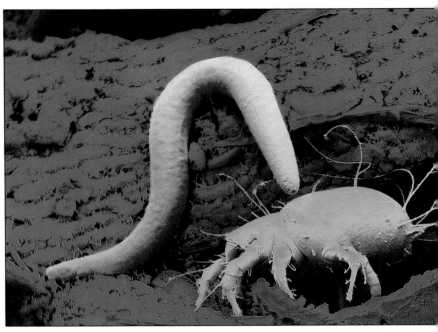

Worm and mite
(x 125)

▶ **In some places, countless numbers of microfossils are buried in the mud at the bottom of the ocean.**

(x 75)

MORE THAN **100** MILLION WORMS, BEETLES, MITES, SLUGS, SNAILS, AND OTHER TINY ANIMALS MAY LIVE IN THE SOIL OF ONE SMALL FIELD.

(x 150)

(x 120)

Microfossils of tiny sea animals

◀ **These microfossils are the remains of tiny sea animals that once lived near the surface of the ocean thousands or even millions of years ago. They were found in the thick layer of mud at the bottom of deep oceans.**

35

GUESS WHAT?

Read the clues, then try to guess what these images are. You'll find the answers at the bottom of the page.

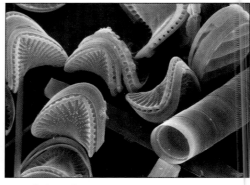

3. Fishy feast? This isn't pasta, but it would make a fine meal for many sea creatures.

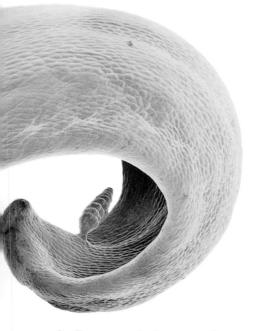

1. All tied up? But in a few days, every bead in this long necklace will make its escape.

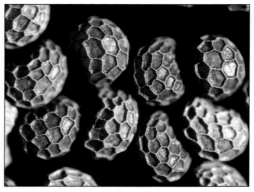

2. Meteorite shower? When these hit the earth, something much prettier than a crater is created.

4. Dragon's tongue? This is inside something that gives off a sweet scent instead of fire and smoke.

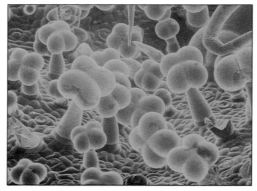

5. Four-leaf clovers? These leaves aren't lucky, but the fruit of this plant tastes great in salad.

6. No bees, please? Actually this honeycomb is part of a stinging plant.

▲ **7. Woodworm?** Is this a beautifully carved chair arm or the face of a wiggly garden creature?

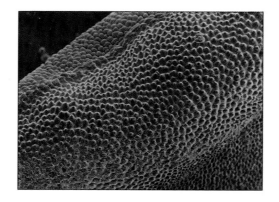

◀ **8. Crocodile skin?** A handbag made from this soft, scented stuff wouldn't last very long!

1. Toad eggs 2. Poppy seeds (x 60) 3. Diatom skeletons (x 500) 4. Female part of hibiscus flower (x 50) 5. Leaf of tomato plant (x 125) 6. Section of nettle stem (x 125) 7. Head of earthworm (x 18) 8. Surface of flower petal (x 90)

Glossary

Amphibians—creatures such as frogs and toads that live both on land and in water. Amphibians usually start life in the water, then move on to land as they mature.

Anther—the swollen tip of each stamen (male part) of a flower, where pollen is made.

Burr—a kind of seed with hooks on it. A burr will attach itself to anything that brushes against it. When the seed eventually falls to the ground, it may grow into a new plant.

Chlorophyll—the chemical that gives leaves their green color. Chlorophyll uses sunlight to turn carbon dioxide gas and water into food that will help the plant grow.

Condensation—the drops of water that form on a cold surface such as a window. Air always contains some water vapor. When air cools down it cannot hold as much water vapor, and some of it is deposited in drops on cold surfaces.

Diatom—a tiny plant that lives in the sea and in freshwater ponds and rivers.

Foraminifera—very small, simple sea animals that live among plankton. Chalky white cliffs are made mainly of foraminifera shells, compressed layer upon layer over millions of years.

Fossil—the remains of a plant or animal, many thousands of years old, that has been turned into stone. Fossils from rocks of different ages can show how life on earth has changed.

Fungus—a kind of plant that feeds on other plants or animals, dead or alive. If a fungus invades another plant, it will gradually eat away at it and spoil it. Some fungi are delicious to eat, but others are deadly poisonous.

Nectar—a sugary liquid produced by some plants and fed on by some birds and insects.

Photosynthesis—the process that allows green plants to make their own food from sunlight, carbon dioxide, and water.

Plankton—tiny, usually microscopic, plants and animals that live just below the surface of the sea. Other creatures, from fish to whales, feed on the plankton.

Pollen—a fine powder produced by the stamens (male parts of flowers) to fertilize the stigmas (female parts).

Pollination—the process of fertilizing seeds in a flower. Most plants need pollen from other plants of the same kind to reproduce, but some can fertilize themselves.

Protozoans—tiny, very simple one-celled animals. Some attach themselves to other living creatures and feed off them.

Spawn—to lay eggs in water, the way fish and frogs do. The eggs are surrounded by a clear protective jelly.

Spores—very small reproductive cells produced by some very simple green plants and fungi. The spores can grow into new plants or fungi.

Stamens—the male parts of a flower, which carry pollen in anthers.

Stigmas—the top parts of the female portion of a flower, which are usually sticky or feathery so they can "catch" pollen grains. The pollen fertilizes the seeds in the flower's ovary.

Vertebrates—creatures with backbones. Fish, reptiles, amphibians, birds, and most mammals (including humans) all have spines made up of small bones called vertebrae.

Water vapor—a gas formed when water warms up and evaporates. There is always some water vapor in the air, even though you cannot see it.

Index

The authors and publishers would like to thank **Andrew Syred** of **Microscopix** and **Liz Hirst** at the **National Institute of Medical Research** for their assistance in the preparation of this book, as well as the other photographers and organizations listed below for their kind permission to reproduce the following photographs:

Dr. Tony Brain: 31 bottom, 35 center, bottom left, and bottom right; **Arthur Burton:** 25 top; **Bruce Coleman:** 36 top left; **Eric Crichton:** 23 right of center; **Liz Hirst/NIMR:** 18 center, 28-29 center, 30 right of center and bottom, 30-31 bottom, 36 below center; **Natural History Museum, London:** 3 right of center, 8 top left, left of center, and bottom left, 17 bottom right, 20 bottom, 26 right of center, 27 center, 29 right—main picture and top right inset; **Nature Photographers/Brinsley Burbidge:** 19 top right and left of center; **NHPA/Anthony Bannister:** 26 bottom; **G. I. Bernard:** 30 top left, above center left, and below center left; **Stephen Dalton:** 30-31 top; **Jeff Goodman:** 29 bottom right inset; **E. A. James:** 18 top; **Oxford Scientific Films/G. I. Bernard:** 24 below center left; **Frederick Ehrenstrom:** 24 bottom far right; **Harry Fox:** 24 above center left; **Peter Parks:** 24 top left, bottom left, and below center; **Reed Consumer Books, Picture Library:** 13 top left; **Science Photo Library/Michael Abbey:** 7 bottom right; **George Bernard:** 17 top right; **Martin Bond:** 22 top left; **Dr. Jeremy Burgess:** 3 bottom left, 8-9 bottom, 9 top left and top right, 10 top left, right of center, and bottom, 10-11 top, 11 top right and bottom right, 12 left, 12-13 center, 13 right of center, 14 top right, 15 left and right, 16 top, bottom left, and bottom right, 17 center, 18 bottom, 20 top right and left of center, 21 top right, center, and bottom left, 32-33 bottom, 34 left of center and bottom left, 35 top right, 36 right of center; **Stevie Grand:** 4 bottom left; **Manfred Kage:** 3 top left, 6 bottom, 7 top left and center, 19 bottom right, 33 bottom right; **Alfred Pasleka:** 33 top right; **Dr. Morley Read:** 28 left; **J. C. Revy:** 29 bottom left; **David Scharf:** 13 bottom right, 22 bottom left and below center, 23 top left, 36 center, bottom left, and bottom right; **Jeremy Trew:** 4 top left; **M. I. Walker:** cover, 25 bottom; **Tony Stone Worldwide/Rex A. Butcher:** 9 left of center; **G. Brad Lewis:** 32 top left; **Ben Osborne:** cover, 14 bottom; **Pete Seaward:** 34 bottom right; **Robin Smith:** 28 center; **Andrew Syred/Microscopix:** 4 top right, right of center, bottom right, and below center, 6 top, 23 bottom, 27 bottom, 31 right of center, 33 above center and left of center, 36 above center and top right.

All illustrations by **Jane Gedye**

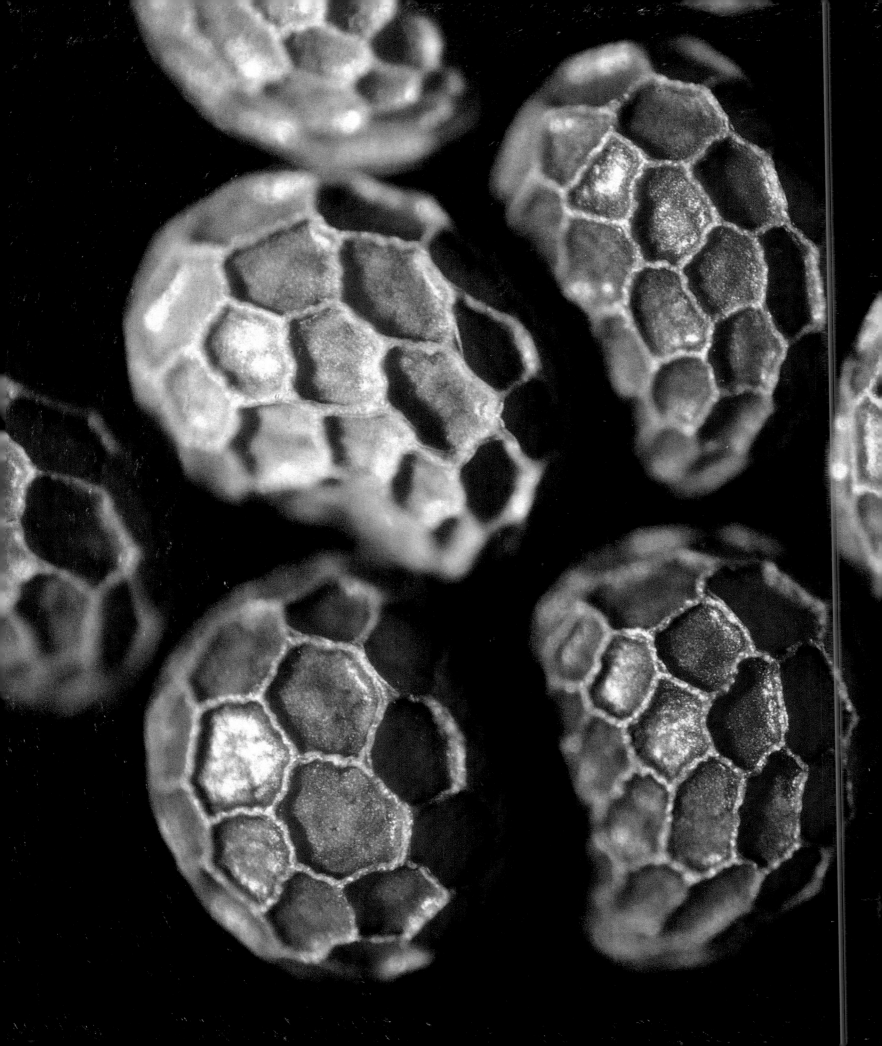